MAY 1 9 2022

WAY PAST LONELY

Hallee Adelman

illustrated by Karen Wall

Albert Whitman & Company
Chicago, Illinois

To Marnee, Jami, Team IBR, and anyone who has felt lonely—HA

To Nina, who makes everyone less lonely—KW

Library of Congress Cataloging-in-Publication data is on file with the publisher.

Text copyright © 2022 by Hallee Adelman
Illustrations copyright © 2022 by Albert Whitman & Company
Illustrations by Karen Wall
First published in the United States of America in 2022 by Albert Whitman & Company
ISBN 978-0-8075-8672-3 (hardcover)
ISBN 978-0-8075-8673-0 (ebook)

Printed in China
10 9 8 7 6 5 4 3 2 1 WKT 26 25 24 23 22 21

Design by Rick DeMonico

For more information about Albert Whitman & Company,
visit our website at www.albertwhitman.com.

After Dez left for the whole weekend,
I didn't know what to do.

Keya couldn't play.
Neither could Hooper.
Even Princess Paws rushed away.
Was *everyone* busy?

"Wanna do something?" I asked Mom.
"One second, honey."
One. Two. Three. Four...
I waited. And waited.

"Can I help?" I asked Luke.
"No, thanks."
Now I felt really lonely.

I decided to go to the playground,
but it was like I was invisible.

I was way past lonely, the kind of lonely that starts like a seed and grows like a weed.

Cai pedaled over from next door.
Maybe he wants to play.
Maybe he'll ask to ride bikes.

Cai stopped and stared straight at me,
and then he just rode away.
I bit my lip.

I hopped on my bike and imagined popping tricks, with Dez, Keya, and Hooper all asking, "Will you teach us?" Mom would be snapping pics, and Princess Paws would be barking at all of us.

The kids from the park would shout,
"Macy, come play with us."
And we'd all play until the sun set.

I rode off on my own,
pushing the pedals real slow.
My loneliness rode with me.
Even the sun stayed away.

I stopped by the stream where
Dez and I always traded rocks
and pretended to be queens, and
I always laughed out loud.

But there was no one to laugh with now.
I was the Queen of Lonely.

I pressed a cold rock into the dirt and wrote four words.

I chucked that rock at the water.

But it didn't sink.
It skip, skip, skipped.
"Woah."

So I grabbed another.
Skip, skip, skip.
And another.
Skip, skip, skip.
I tipped to my toes and smiled.
I felt better. "This queen needs a crown."

I gathered sticks and weeds and leaves.

I sat on my giant throne,
swinging my legs and humming in tune with the water.
Being alone felt good.
Maybe I could be my own friend.

The ducks quacked. I hurried toward them, quacking back and laughing.

I raced the stream to the tall tree and won! "Yipee!"
I saw Dez's note.
A big smile stretched across my face.
Dez was away, and everyone was busy,
but I still had me. I didn't feel so lonely now.

But someone else looked like he was.

I pedaled over. "Wanna teach me some bike tricks?"
"Really?" said Cai. "Sure!"

I cheered Cai on
until he was ready for his own crown.

Then we rode past lonely,

and we played until the sun set.